Benjamin Dilley's THiRSTY CAMEL

by
Jolly Roger Bradfield

Rand Mc Nally & Company
CHICAGO   NEW YORK   SAN FRANCISCO

Benjamin Dilley was a little boy about the same age as most little boys. People said that Benjamin Dilley was a dreamer; but the truth was that he had a *wonderful imagination*. For instance, he could shut his eyes and imagine a lavender hippopotamus in a general's uniform smelling a flower, and when he opened his eyes . . .

. . . there would be the hippo!

Really.

A real, live hippopotamus in a general's uniform standing right there in front of Benjamin.

He could imagine a genie in a bottle...

Or out of a bottle.

And that genie was so real that he'd even
grant Benjamin a wish.

Benjamin Dilley could see almost *anything*
with that wonderful imagination of his.
A goat driving a sports car . . .

Bunnies jumping on the furniture . . .

Or a scarey witch doctor jumping rope
with a snake!

Once he even imagined a friendly whale
that took him clear around the world one morn-
ing, swimming so fast that Benjamin got back
in plenty of time to wash his hands for lunch!

The trouble was that nobody but Benjamin could *see* all these wonderful things.

Benjamin would say, "Mom, you shouldn't work so hard—my genie would be GLAD to do that."

But his mother would say, "Yes, dear, that's nice. Keep off the floor 'til it's dry, won't you, dear."

Benjamin would say, "Look, Grandpa, there's a whole platoon of soldiers standing right behind you!"

But Grandpa would just say, "That reminds me of the time I was in the army." And then he'd tell Benjamin all about it. Again.

Benjamin would say, "Dad! Have you ever seen a turtle in a turtleneck sweater?"

But Father would just say, "No, I haven't. Have you seen the rest of my paper?"

One afternoon Benjamin Dilley was watching his father fix a leak in a pipe down in their basement. It was a small leak—just a

drip now and then—but it was taking Benjamin's father a long time. (His wrench was 'way too big, for one thing.)

To pass the time, Benjamin imagined a funny old camel with glasses perched on the end of his nose.

They decided to have a game of Ping-Pong while Father worked. The camel looked quite old and rickety, but he turned out to be a very good Ping-Pong player.

"My camel says you're turning that wrench the wrong way, Dad," said Benjamin.

"Your father knows what he's do—," his father started to say. But a great gush of water interrupted him, squirting from the pipe with a frightening sound!

All over Father.

And Benjamin.

And the basement floor.

Benjamin's father struggled with the pipe, but it was no use. He just got wetter. And he dropped his wrench.

The water kept spraying out of the pipe, and spreading out over the basement floor. Soon it was an inch deep. And then two inches. In no time it reached almost to Father's knees!

"It's a regular FLOOD!" he cried. Letting go of the pipe, he splashed to the stairs and dashed up to the kitchen.

Benjamin Dilley could hear his father shouting into the telephone, "HELP! Send a plumber over right away! Send TWO plumbers! And *hurry!*"

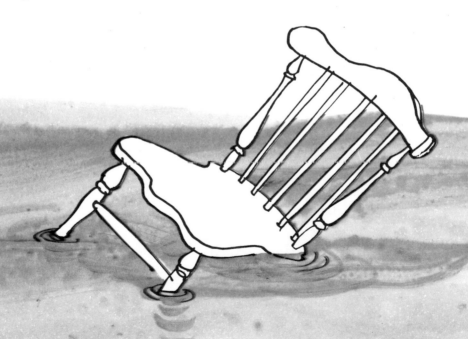

Benjamin looked at the water rising around his tummy.

"DO something, Mr. Camel!" he shouted.

"Glad to," said the camel.

First he found Father's big wrench. Using it to turn the pipe (the opposite way that Father had), he managed to stop the frightening rush of water almost at once. Then he did a remarkable thing. . . .

He started to drink.
He drank and he drank.
He kept *on* drinking.
"Delicious water you have here," he said between gulps. The skinny old camel started to fill out. He reminded Benjamin of a balloon being blown up. With each gulp he grew wider and taller. His two humps even grew fatter!

Soon the basement was almost completely dry. The camel was licking up the last few drops under the Ping-Pong table when both Father and Mother came rushing down the stairs, carrying mops and pails.

Mother was crying, "My baby! He'll drown!"

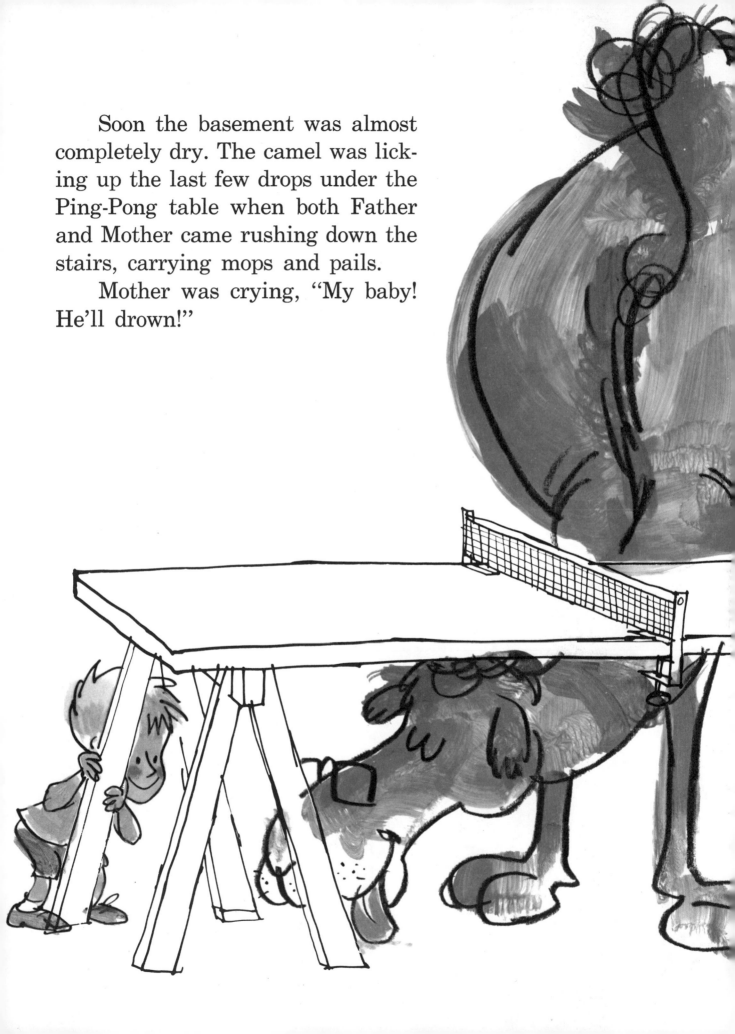

"Everything's under control," said the camel quietly.

Benjamin Dilley's father didn't hear him. "The water's GONE!" he cried. "I don't understand."

"Naturally," said the camel. "I drank—"

But of course Father didn't hear. "I just don't understand!" he repeated.

And the next minute, the plumber was banging on the kitchen door.

The plumber was a big man in blue overalls. He was followed by two helpers carrying tools.

"Where's the flood?" he shouted.

"It's gone," said Father.

"My camel drank it up!" explained Benjamin, but no one paid any attention to him.

The plumber looked around at the dry basement. "I thought you said it was filling up with water," he grumbled.

Benjamin thought he sounded a little disappointed.

Finally, after searching in corners and behind things, the plumber found a small drain under the washtubs. He scratched his head, and said that somehow the water must have all gone down that little drain.

"Of course," said Father.

"Of course," said Mother.

And that was that.

It seemed impossible to Benjamin that none of the plumbers noticed his camel. Camels are all pretty big, and this one, with all that water in him, was the fattest, bulgiest one ever.

Benjamin thought that if the plumber was able to see that tiny drain under the washtubs, he should be able to see a great big camel!

Just to check, he imagined a whole tree full of owls right in front of the plumber. The plumber didn't see them.

Benjamin imagined a horse, playing a trombone just as loud as he could—right into the ear of one of the helpers.

The helper didn't see it.

Or hear it.

Finally he imagined a leprechaun, who danced merrily around the basement painting everyone blue.

But they didn't notice.
Not even Mother, who always
said that blue was her favorite color.

When the plumbers had left, Benjamin Dilley's father gave a sigh of relief. "Well, *that* was lucky! If that little drain hadn't worked so well, all that water would have really made a mess!"

Benjamin patted the camel. "Don't you care," he whispered. "*I* know you did it."

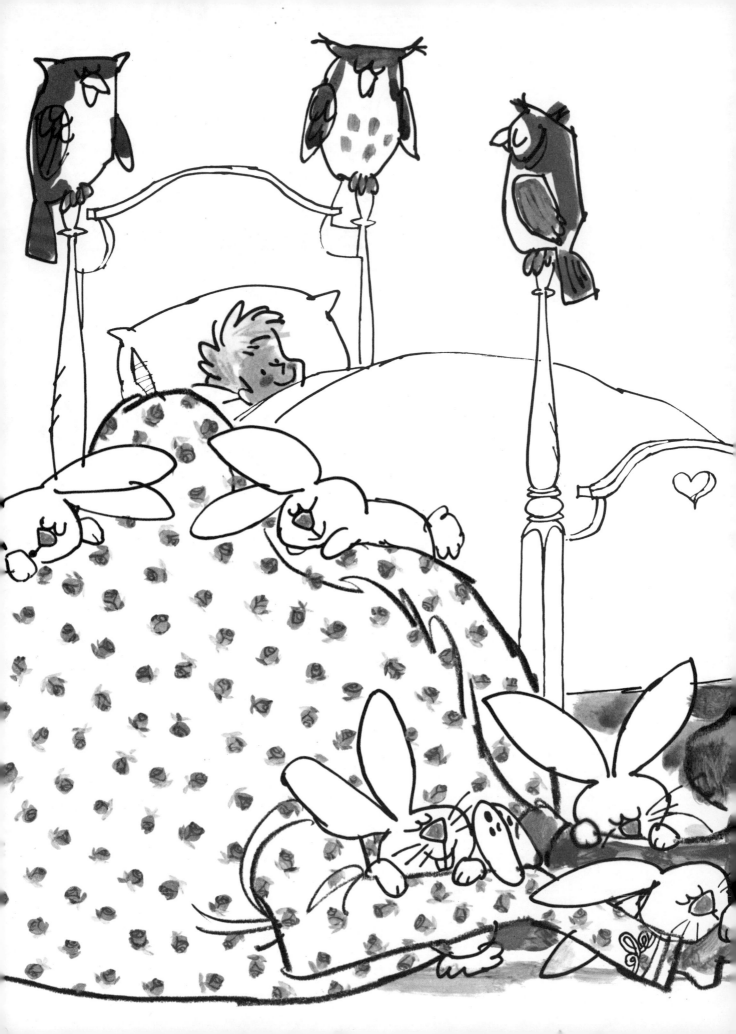

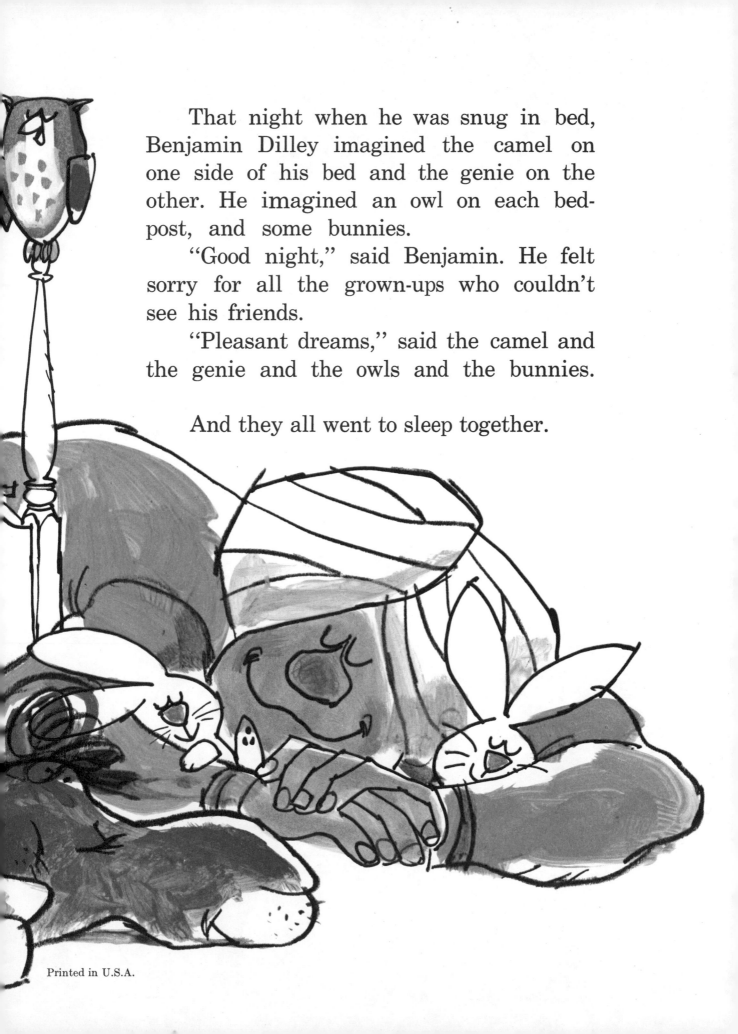

That night when he was snug in bed, Benjamin Dilley imagined the camel on one side of his bed and the genie on the other. He imagined an owl on each bedpost, and some bunnies.

"Good night," said Benjamin. He felt sorry for all the grown-ups who couldn't see his friends.

"Pleasant dreams," said the camel and the genie and the owls and the bunnies.

And they all went to sleep together.